A Kiss Is The Secret

AMY LAURENS

OTHER WORKS

Find other works by the author at www.amylaurens.com

A Kiss Is The Secret

INKLET #60

AMY LAURENS

Inkprint PRESS

www.inkprintpress.com

Print ISBN: 978-1-925825-62-6
eBook ISBN: 9781393847533

www.inkprintpress.com

National Library of Australia Cataloguing-in-Publication Data
Laurens, Amy 1985 –
A Kiss Is The Secret
68 p.
ISBN: 978-1-925825-62-6
Inkprint Press, Canberra, Australia
1. Fiction—Fantasy—Contemporary 2. Fiction—Fantasy—Romantic 3. Fiction—Short Stories

First Print Edition: June 2021
Cover photo © Free-Photos via Pixabay
Cover design © Inkprint Press
Interior art © Amy Laurens

A KISS IS THE SECRET

A KISS IS THE SECRET, MY MOTHER always said, and it made absolutely not a jot of sense to me for the longest of times. She'd grown up in a convent, you see; not a nun herself—obviously, because me—but with the nuns, raised by them, for she had no idea who her parents were.

Well, that's ungenerous. She knew exactly who they were; the nuns were kind in that respect. But her parents had no idea who she was, nor any desire to know; they, unlike the nuns, were not kind.

So, my mother grew up in a convent, where as a rule there is not a whole lot of kissing, unless of course it is the mother superior's ring, or something like that.

Do they kiss the mother superior's ring? I'm not even sure.

But regardless, there were no boys in the convent, and Mother was never allowed off the grounds except under strict supervision, and so naturally there wasn't much kissing of the real sort in her life.

I used to think perhaps that she meant a kiss was the reason she'd left the convent; a secret kiss, stolen opportunistically in a private moment from my father, whom of course she ran away and married.

But secrets are never that straightforward.

For a happy interlude, they thought that nothing was wrong. They eloped, bought a house with my father's savings, started a little cheese-making business with three sheep and five cows and a goat, and by all accounts were very, very happy.

Then they had me.

Now, don't get me wrong. Neither of my parents ever insinuated for the slightest of moments that I brought them anything but the usual delight of a baby (which is to say, a fair bit of frustration and the distinct possibility of momentary loathing, all under-scored by a whole lot o' love).

And for a while, that was true.

But one day, much later on, they discovered that I'd brought with me into the world rather a lot more than your average ordinary baby.

Mother hadn't realised at the time —thought I can hardly imagine she didn't *know*, at least on some level—

but the nuns she grew up with belonged to a very particular order: a magical order.

It wasn't the kind of magic you flaunted around, making things fly and turning these things into those. No. This was a quiet magic, the deep, old magic of the natural world: the magic of life.

True enough, they were all greenthumbs, and to hear my mother describe it, living in the convent had been like growing up part wood elf: the passageways lined with moss paintings on the grey, stone walls, every sunlit alcove an altar to something green and frondy, hanging baskets endangering everyone's heads at every door, the entire courtyard one living, pulsing forest of greenery, a homage to nature.

The whole place smelled like sap and stone, and when it rained, my mother said, the petrichor fairly took your breath away.

But it was more than just a proclivity for growing things too; more than just green thumbs. That's wondrous, to be sure, but not, in the truest sense, magical.

Or at least, not magical enough that it would disrupt my life—or Vincent's.

You see, Vincent's mother had also been at the convent, though for a much briefer time than my mother: four years before my mother met my father and ran away and got married and had the audacity to birth a baby only six months later, another woman stayed at the convent, some fifteen years my mother's senior, and heavily with child. Heavy with child, heavy with exhaustion, and heavy with bruises, my mother always said.

Poor thing.

Of course, when I met Vincent in the woods that night, neither of us had any idea of the connection our parents shared—or of our shared link to the magical nuns—and each other.

Well, maybe that last we knew: I was nineteen and fancied myself world-weary, too fashionably cynical for love-at-first-sight, too bound up in my university education to remember there were things like magic in the world. I'd only gone walking in the woods that night beneath the silver-barked birches with their yellowing leaves and the light of a near-full moon because I'd been crammed indoors all day studying, and ten p.m. was the first time my body deigned to remind me that curving my spine over books all day was not conducive to good health and prosperity.

So I'd been walking through woods that smelled of damp leaf litter and rotting wood, the trickling of a small brook in my right ear, the moon over my left shoulder, when I'd seen a man up ahead, his back turned to me, pale hair dusted silver in the moonlight.

He was staring up at the sky—at the stars—with such an expression of beatific rapture that I nearly turned back the way I'd come so as to leave him in peace.

But something deep inside my chest stirred at the sight of him, something I'd forgotten being at university, away from home, away from my mother's tales of creeping vines and old stonework, of the prayerful hands of hushed nuns smoothing over the bodies of the dead and restoring life (I could never quite divine from my mother's tales whether these dead were human bodies, or simply dry, withered plants the nuns seemed to bring back from the dead, though I have my suspicions).

Regardless, that something stirred in my chest like a sleeping dragon opening one eyelid, and instead of backing away down the path, I found myself striding toward this strange man in the night, fists clenched at my sides as I wondered what I was doing and if perhaps I was going to end up hurt.

The man—Vincent—turned to face me, and I saw that the stars were no longer in the sky, but rather were in his eyes.

My breath caught as I saw Venus rise and set in his irises, watched Mars glimmer and fade away. There was magic in the world, to be sure, and it was concentrated here, in this strange man.

He held his hand out to me, and energy crackled over his fingertips—or at least, I imagined it did, and I imagined it so vividly, in full, splendid, viridian colour that it might as well have done.

I took his hand, and I know what you are thinking: there, under the moonlight, we kissed, and that was what my mother had been talking about—to which I respond, we did no such thing. That there is magic in the world, that I am part of it, does not give me licence to be naïve.

No. We did not kiss, not that first night, nor for many more, but we did talk. It eventuated that Vincent was attending my very own university, though half a degree ahead of me— only half, for he had chopped and changed a number of times before settling on philosophy.

I think it was the second night I asked him what exactly he proposed to do for a living, how precisely it was that he intended for philosophy to pay the bills.

He grinned at me, teeth nearly as bright as his starlit eyes, and told me that that was precisely the reason he intended to marry someone like my-self: someone practical, in a guaran-teed field of employment, who could sustain his quixotic ways.

I, of course, scoffed, thinking that this—merely an accidental moonlit tryst—could hardly be trusted to turn into something so stolid as marriage.

Three months later, my mother died. My father rang to say she was ill, but by the time I made it home, she was gone. She'd slipped from the world with a minimum of fuss, simply waking unwell one morning, losing strength and colour and body mass by that evening so that father thought to call me, and drifting away in her sleep some time during the night.

Quietly, quickly, decisively, and with a minimum of fuss: that was my mother, her convent upbringing showing like the stubborn grey streak in her hair that even permanent dyes could only hide for a matter of weeks.

If I'd been there sooner, perhaps I could have saved her.

She'd left a message for me, of course, but it was merely a reiteration of the same enigmatic epigram she'd been reciting to me since we all mutually realised at nine that I was Not Like Other Children: A kiss is the secret.

A kiss is the secret, a kiss is the secret. How I loathed that phrase. I shredded the paper she'd written it on into confetti and threw it all over the kitchen floor in a fit of pique, storming out of the house to phone Vincent— who in the space of the last three months had become an invaluable source of solace.

He offered to come up for the funeral, but I declined, reminding him that it was difficult to pass exams that one was not present for, and that, while I had an excuse, it being a family member who had died, he could hardly write on an application for extension that the mother of his 'what even are we is this dating or are we just friends' had passed away.

(I said it matter-of-factly, because the fact of the matter was we *didn't* know what it was at that point, his ardent declarations aside.)

It was at the creek in the woods behind my house on the day following the funeral that I touched, for the first time since about age fifteen, the strain of magic energy that ran somehow through my veins as I stood under the canopy of blushing aspens and gilded oaks, listening to the creek flow past—noisier than the one near campus, wider, shallower, full of rocks and white foam, scented like all good fresh water should be.

I remembered what it had felt like, that time when I'd been nine, and I'd helped my mother plant a garden out the back of the house, plunging my hands wrist-deep into thick, black dirt, spiking seeds into the ground with a fingertip, teeny tiny daisy seeds and large, eye-like sun-flower seeds and the spherical, dark brown seeds of cabbages.

I hadn't wanted to help, had resented the dirt crusting beneath my nails and the time spent away from my books, but better, perhaps, that it had happened then that at some other inopportune moment.

For in the morning, the cabbages had been as large as my head—larger, even, than the sunflower heads, which bobbed merrily with their red-and-yellow frills at the sun some four feet above the gutters of the house, while cheery yellow and white daisies carpeted their feet. Pollen drifted in the air, catching in the back of my throat in an acrid, green kind of way.

Mother had looked at me then, with wonder in her eyes and not even the slightest trace of fear (to her credit), her fingertips brushing her lips as she stared. "You have it too," she whispered, then went on to tell me—for the first time in any definite sort of way—of the way she'd seen things grow in the convent, nuns trailing their fingertips over baby vines which hastily unspooled and lengthened, following the hands of their human caretakers. She'd seen, in mere hours, acorns turn to oaks, tomatoes blossom and swell with fruit first lime-ish green before blushing through to red, perfuming the air with their sweet, sharp invitation.

The tales she'd told me all my life of the green-encrusted nunnery took on a different sheen.

"You have it too," she'd said, cupping my face in her hands, brushing my hair back from my forehead as tenderly as a feather. She kissed my forehead gently. "You have it too."

A day later, the plants had withered and died.

It was not long after that that Mother began her oft-mentioned refrain: A kiss is the secret, a kiss is the secret.

It made as little sense to me then as it did now, and Mother had been unable to elaborate on her meaning, stating only that it was a mantra she'd learned at the convent, that she knew it was important for me to know, but that she had not the slightest sense of understanding why.

So I'd put the magic away, rarely touched it except as a passing curiosity for my eyes, and mine alone (I'd learned already that in middle school, 'special' is just a synonym for 'outcast'). The last time I'd touched it was not long after I'd turned fifteen, right here under these aspens and these oaks, with the smell of leaf mould all around and the fat creek laughing. I'd dared to show a friend—a boy, in fact, whom I'd rather hoped might become *more* than a friend.

He ran screaming as the emerald grass shot up around him, ivy winding up trees before our eyes, dandelions bursting into puff balls that drifted away on the wind.

The accelerated growth had killed the plants before I'd finished crying. Clearly, whatever it was my mother thought her nuns had had, I did not 'have it too'.

And so I'd locked this strange peculiarity of mine away, never touching it since then.

But today... Today I was letting it out again. I touched the touch bark of the oak on my right and let all my grief, all my insecurities, the quiet *longing* of my soul that I'd managed to stifle but never gag flow out into the tree, a trickle that fast became a torrent rising from deep within me.

I screamed, because it was the only place in life where I could do so without fear of being heard, shouting into the emptiness of the forest the emptiness my mother's passing had left inside.

The tree turned black almost at once, as though it had been burned alive.

Ash pattered down in the breeze, and the air smelled of charcoal, of the faintest hint of woodsmoke.

I jerked away from the tree, astounded, terrified—guilt-ridden. Here was evidence once more of the uselessness—nay, the wanton destructiveness—of my 'talent'.

I called Vincent that night. I told him we shouldn't see each other any more, that whatever our relationship had been, it had been made of starshine and magic, and neither of those bore up well in the cold, harsh light of day.

He laughed at me, told me that if this was how I needed to grieve, then that was fine by him. He'd be there, waiting, when I returned.

I returned. A week later, I headed back to university to sit my delayed exams and, true to his word, Vincent met me at the station. I spotted him through the maze of people, locked eyes with his night-blue ones, strode to him through people barely more relevant to me at that moment than posts.

My jaw twitched as I clenched it.

I reached him; he started to speak.

I grabbed him firmly, one hand to his cheek, the other to the back of his neck, and kissed him. Hard.

There was nothing.

He reeled back, astonished, in the moment it took for my heart to sink the last of the way through my feet and into the cold, hard concrete below.

Stupid. Stupid to think that one kiss could be any kind of secret, could be any kind of balm for the sorrow I was facing.

I packed my things. Transferred immediately to a different university, a citified one, right in the middle of three million people with bricks and concrete and scarcely a blade of grass to be seen.

Vincent called me: five, seven, nine, twelve times a day to begin with, then four, then three, then none. In his defence, most people would have given up after the first six weeks, when I refused to take his calls or return his messages.

I was done with magic, and anything and anyone who stank of it.

What good had it done me in my life after all? Bullied and outcast, I hadn't even been able to scrape together enough life to save my own mother.

My father didn't mind, of course. That I'd transferred universities, that I never came to see him, that I avoided the family house like the plague… None of it mattered to a mind cast mute by grief. He went through his daily motions, milking his sheep and his cows and his goats, turning his cheese, selling them mutely to passersby to pay the bills—but he was every bit as empty as I was full, and what I was full of was determination that I would never, ever again be lured in by the promise of *more*.

Until one day, six months later, when a postcard arrived at my door.

I say 'at my door', and I mean that quite literally, for I was now living in the student accommodation on campus, and all our mail was sorted for us and delivered by floor, and our floor held the friendly little tradition that whenever one passed the communal mailbox, one was duty bound to select three items from it and see them delivered to the correct rooms.

The postcard bore a garish caricature of a pair of lips, and I nearly mistook it for trash and binned the thing immediately—but as I flipped it over, a hasty scrawl on the back caught my attention.

I knew that handwriting.

As it transpired, the garish postcard was indeed a piece of advertising—for the spring-time opening of a new club down on the city strip, crammed elbow-to-elbow between a corner grocery store and a Chinese restaurant and no doubt stinking of cigarette smoke and beer.

But Vincent had scrawled on the corner—and I was sure it was Vincent, his handwriting may as well have been etched on my skin—"See you at 6." and a big love heart, which was the primary part that made me doubt the writing his after all. Philosophy majors, in my experience, were not terribly prone to signing love hearts.

Then again, perhaps he'd been studying Sartre this term.

I admit, I was curious to see what had changed Vincent so, for he knew full well that such as place as this was the last on a very long list of places I cared never to frequent—and if my memory served me correctly, he hadn't been overly fond of such places himself. Philosophy, he'd told me, preferred bookstores to bottleshops.

And so, wondering what it was that had lured him to such a place, and that was now luring me through him into its grasp, dutifully, I went as summoned. I'd had to borrow an outfit from my neighbour, for the raciest thing I had in my wardrobe was the knee-length, boat-necked black dress I'd worn to Mother's funeral, and I refused to sully that in the name of curiosity.

(Also, I did have *some* sense of clubbing decorum, enough to know that it requisited rather a lot more *skin*.)

I stepped through the doorway into a haze of smoke that didn't smell entirely like cigarettes and wafted it impatiently from my face. A futile attempt, since there was ample more smoke waiting to take its place, but I felt the need to do it anyway in an attempt to delineate my personal space.

Vincent was sitting at the bar on a stool, pale hair strobing from lilac to sky to viridian courtesy of the dance floor's lighting, mid-conversation with the pretty brunette on his left.

I couldn't hear what they were saying until I was practically on top of them, such was the volume around me—some conversational chatter (I assumed), but largely the contribution of the over-enthusiastic bass line on the noise I supposed might generously pass for music.

Honestly, the whole thing put me in a grouchy frame of mind, exacerbating the thing I'd been trying diligently to ignore since moving here: that in this city, at this university, out of the way of all things rural and most things green, my mood and mental health had been gradually declining.

"So," I said, taking the seat on Vincent's other side without a care for the fact that I was interrupting his conversation. "Tell me why I'm here?"

With a closing nod to his prior companion, Vincent swivelled to me and smiled. In this lighting, his eyes may as well have been black. "I brought you something," he said.

"Oh?" My eyebrow arched, and even I wasn't sure if it was contempt or curiosity.

He retrieved a brown paper bag that had been sitting at his feet, lifting it gently onto the bar.

The brunette on his other side had gone back to her drink happily enough when I'd interrupted, but now she—like me, though I was loathe to admit it—leaned a little toward Vincent, the promise of mystery luring us in.

With two careful hands, Vincent withdrew a plant from the bag.

Brunette sniffed inaudibly in the noise and turned back to her vibrant blue cocktail.

I, on the other hand, froze.

He knew, of course, about my penchant for plants; we'd discussed the strange coincidence of our mothers' both having spent time at the convent, had debated back and forth in the moonlight the meaning of our mothers' tales of the nuns' strange abilities.

I'd never once, though, told him that I had inherited those abilities.

And now he showed up, out of the infinite blue, in the last place I desired to be, with a potted aloe.

My mouth wrinkled in disgust and I pushed the pot—lapis-glazed ceramic—back at him. "No," I said. "Thank you."

He smiled gently. "You should take it," he said. "I think it will help."

I narrowed my eyes at him. "I don't need help."

"Of course not," he said, with that same gentle smile.

Uncharacteristically, I had the urge to punch his face. I stood, attempting to siphon off some of my sudden excess of energy. My jaw twitched.

Vincent leaned back casually, tipping his head to rest on his hand, elbow propped on the bar by the paper bag. "I still love you, you know."

The thump-thump-thump of the bass was suddenly and implausibly drowned out by my heartbeat. I snatched up the plant. "Thanks."

Aloe cradled in the crook of one arm, I strode from the den of smoke and stupidity, intending never to see him again.

Fate, of course, had other plans—and other plants, for they began turning up in the dorm floor's mailbox with alarming regularity, until the entire third floor knew me as Plant Girl, or, in their less generous moments, Pothead. Two months on with the year's finals fast approaching, my little room was fairly overflowing with them—but no matter how much I railed against Vincent's stubborn persistence, no matter how the rest of the student body snickered, I couldn't bring myself to throw a single one away.

It goes without saying that, in the dim, dry confines of my dorm room, the plants nonetheless flourished. A spider plant now larger than my head hung from the roof above the little desk, striated leaves casting long, slatted shadows on the floor. A collection of cacti covered the bookcase, hiding the spines of the books with their own dazzling array of spines and orange flowers. Air plants colonised the wall over my bed; a row of snake plants lined the splash back behind my tiny kitchenette sink; trailing philodendrons covered the small windowsill. The piece de resistance was a ficus tree in a pot larger than my desk chair, which had taken three students to haul from the mail area to my room. I didn't know what to make of them.

Mostly, I ignored the plants. Tried to pretend that they were there by my invitation, that their presence was meaningless apart from some air-purifying decoration that made my room seem less like a prison cell and more like a place of residence. Tried to pretend that my correlative boost in mood and health was coincidence, a result of my becoming more comfortable and familiar with my new place of study.

Never once did I attempt to help their growth. It simply wasn't worth the risk.

They did keep growing though, and despite periods of neglect—particularly when the exams did roll around again—not a one of them ever sickened, let alone died.

It was the last day of the schooling year that things changed. I had finally come to terms with the fact that I would be required to pack up my room and take everything home for the holidays, but had yet to devise a means both plausible and practical of transporting my miniature forest home. The little gardenia bush, the most recent addition, was flowering away on my desk, perfuming the air with its light, sweet floral fragrance, and between the greenery and my suitcases it appeared for all the world as though I'd decided to take a jaunty holiday in a rainforest.

But I had to catch the train home, and there was simply no feasible way to manage bringing all the plants with me.

I tried to pretend it didn't matter—but as I collected my diary with the train tickets off my desk and prepared to leave, my gaze fell on the ridiculous ad for the club opening that Vincent had sent me a couple of months ago, tucked into the frame of the corkboard above the desk. The magenta lips were as lurid as ever, a beacon in the dim lighting of the room with its insufficient lightbulb.

I sighed. It did matter, and I would miss the little plants he had sent me more than I cared to say.

Luck, however, was on my side, for at that precise moment, there was a gentle knock at the door.

I placed my diary back down on the desk, dropped the suitcase, and headed to the door, gently but absently brushing back the fronds of the pothos plant that were threatening to encroach on the door space.

"Hello?"

The woman who stood in front of me was barely familiar, another student from my biology classes whose curly bleached hair and ready smile saw her often in the centre of friendly, admiring attention.

Clee-something. Cleotha, that was it.

"Hi." Cleotha flashed me her smile, and I pretended to regard her with something other than detachment. "How are you getting home?"

"Train," I said simply, which bothered her not in the slightest, for everyone on my floor was well acquainted by now with my verbal brevity.

"How are you managing the pots?"

I shrugged a shoulder. "Uncertain at present."

Her smile broadened to a grin. Briefly, I wondered what such an expression might look like on me. "I'll take them," she said.

I raised my eyebrows, leaning against the wooden doorframe.

"You live in West Caymare, right?"

I nodded.

"My boyfriend is in Langbrinx, and I'm heading there for Christmas. I can bring your plants."

I scrutinised her face for any sign of teasing—but there was none to be found. The offer, as far as I could tell, was genuine. I smiled back. "Thank you," I said. "I would appreciate that. A lot."

Cleotha grinned again, teeth white against the brown of her skin. "Just leave your room unlocked when you go," she said. "I'll come get them when Kingston gets here."

I nodded. "Thank you."

She threw me a joyful little wave over her shoulder as she retreated down the hall.

I closed the door. I leaned against it.

The bed had been stripped bare, the kitchenette emptied of all personal items. The desk was clear, and the bookcase held only dust and pots.

But the room was still full, lush and green and smelling of sap and leaves and potting mix and a little hint of fertiliser.

And I wouldn't have to leave my plants behind. I wouldn't, some small part of me piped up, have to leave Vincent behind.

I sniffed and pushed that thought aside, retrieving my diary once more from the desk, my suitcase once more from the floor.

I turned back to the door.

Deep breath. Now was not the time for sentimentality.

Still. I smiled at the pothos with its glossy, heart-shaped leaves as I shuffled my diary under my arm and reached for the door. The pothos tickled my face, and impulsively, I raised my chin to it, allowing it to brush my cheeks.

It wouldn't hurt to say goodbye, I thought.

Perhaps they do understand after all.

So before I opened the door, I reached up and took a pothos leaf in hand. It was thick and glossy, smooth and shiny. "Goodbye," I whispered to it. "Thank you for cleaning my air."

I kissed the leaf of the plant.

I left.

A week later, Cleotha appeared on my home doorstep, and somewhat uncharacteristically for me, I was pleased to see her. Vincent, it seemed, had given up on me at last, for although he had to know I'd gone home for the holidays, there'd been no plants, no junk mail summons—and no phone calls.

It surprised me, the morning I realised I'd been expecting one. He hadn't called in months; why should he start now?

I tried to put the idea from my mind, but with naught but the goat and the cows and my taciturn father, there was little for it to do but grow. And so I welcomed Cleotha perhaps more heartily than I might have otherwise done.

She simply laughed when I embraced her, hugging me back with simple, unconstrained warmth, then led me around to the grey gravel drive where her boyfriend waited in the car—an SUV, thank goodness, with ample room in the back seat to stand my ficus tree.

In my relief at seeing the ficus upright and in good health, I failed to notice what should have at once been apparent: that the car was fairly overflowing with plants, with barely room for the driver and his passenger at all.

I blinked. "How did you even drive?"

Cleotha laughed. "I don't know what you were feeding that one," she said, pointing to the long, trailing tendrils of pothos invading the front of the car, "but I swear it's grown about three feet since we loaded it in the car this morning."

Something inside me twisted. I said no more, but instead hurried to help them unload the plants onto the front verandah.

"Thank you," I said, pulling a twenty from my pocket and offering it.

Cleotha laughed it away. "Honestly," she said. "It's no trouble at all. I always thought I'd like to be your friend."

I regarded her for a fraction too long before realising she was serious. I smiled. "Thank you," I said again. "I'd like that."

She nodded. "It's not good to isolate yourself so much, you know?"

I nodded back as though I agreed, and they pulled out of the drive and away, and I walked back to the verandah alone.

I could call Vincent.

I shook my head. I'd put him aside long ago, and one silly encounter with a woman doing me a favour oughtn't to change that.

There *was* the matter of the pothos, though. While all the other plants seemed healthy enough despite our one-week separation, the pothos had done more than survived: it had flourished.

Cleotha had barely been exaggerating: the plant was well over-growing its pot, easily four times the size it had been when I'd seen it last.

My stomach twisted. Something deep in my chest twanged.

There was only one thing that the pothos had received that the others had not.

Pulse pitter-pattering, I bent toward it. The earthy smell of its potting soil enveloped me—and I pressed my lips to a leaf.

As I did, adrenalin sparked through me—and into the plant. It was a familiar feeling, one I'd felt several times before: the feeling of that magic, whatever it was, leaving my body—and passing into the pothos.

Its tendrils grew three inches.

I forgot how to breathe.

I'd made it grow. I'd made it grow, and it hadn't died, hadn't disintegrated into dust, hadn't wilted and wasted and given up on its life in the world.

A kiss, Mother had said, is the secret.

I sat on the front step, the concrete cold through my thin cotton skirt, and rummaged through my memories.

I'd resented being in the garden that day with my mother. I'd been terrified the time I'd tried to impress the boy. Grieving when I'd burned the oak to ash. Try as I might, I couldn't remember a single instance of using my gift where I'd been happy enough to use it—where I'd been clear-headed and joyful-hearted, thinking only of the plant and its needs as I tried to help it grow.

A kiss. A kiss was indeed the secret. My mother, bless her, had been right.

I leaned over and caught up the aloe that had been Vincent's first gift. I ran a finger carefully down one leaf, for I knew that although humans appreciated the tactile experience of touch, it could stunt a plant so easily.

A kiss, though?

I leaned down, the lapis-blue pot cradled in my lap.

I inhaled the aloe scent, the sharp bite of fertiliser. I touched my lips, feather light, to the plant. *I do love you.*

The plant grew, leaves lengthening, a tiny baby aloe sprouting into existence at the base of the plant.

I smiled.

"I knew you'd come around."

I startled upright, meeting Vincent's eyes with a heart that beat too wildly for words.

I swallowed, fingers clutching the smooth, comforting weight of the aloe pot. "I hoped you would."

Gently, he took the aloe from me, and set it on the step. "I told you I wouldn't give up," he said.

"I'm glad," I said.

He smiled—and we kissed. It was a very good kiss, and suddenly I regretted all the kisses we might have had in all the months since I'd left, had I not been so stubborn, and so foolish.

"So," he said as he pulled away. "Are you ready to marry me and pay my bills yet?"

"I am twenty years old," I told him sternly with a frown. "And I'm not naïve."

Vincent laughed. "Fine," he said. "We'll wait. But I hope this time you'll let me wait with you."

I regarded him, his dark blue eyes

dancing, his pale hair curling around his ears. "I think," I said, "that I would like that very much."

He hugged me tight. "*I'm* glad."

"Thank you for the plants."

"You're welcome," he said. "I'm glad you figured it out."

I leaned back from him and frowned again. "What do you mean?"

He laughed again, bent down, and kissed the aloe. A stalk sprouted from its middle, blossoming into a head of red, bell-shaped flowers.

I took him by the hand, his fingers laced in mine. "Come on," I said. "I want to show you the garden."

THE MAKING OF
A KISS IS THE SECRET

This story took a long time to birth. While the opening arrived easily enough, I put it away for over two years before the rest of the story deigned to follow.

All I knew from the start was that the kiss wouldn't be a traditional romantic kiss. That, and that the plants were slightly magical in some way.

Everything else I unearthed laboriously, one sentence at a time, never quite getting a glimpse of the entirety of the story until it was actually *done*. Every time I thought I'd had a breakthrough (going, "Ah ha! NOW we are nearly at the end of the story! The kiss will surely happen soon and we will be

DONE!"), the story fooled me and twisted aside, shying away from that kiss that I was desperate to untangle, to uncover, to understand.

So I guess, in a lot of ways, the process of writing this story actually mimicked the experiences of the protagonist: she too spent years getting close to answers and then falling away again, nearly understanding before having it slip through her fingers like water, before finally, *finally*, stumbling in a quiet, accidental moment on the answer.

Does art mimic life, or does life mimic art?

A silly question, of course, because the answer is: both.

(Also, can I please have some magic plants?)

Read more by Amy Laurens!

DREAMING OF FORESTS

THERE WAS A FOREST. THAT WAS THE simple fact of the matter: there was a forest now, and there hadn't been before. Deena let the tent flap drop closed in front of her, inhaled steadily, and tried again.

Nope, still forest. She bit her lip, debating: go out and explore, or hide in the tent?

In the end, exploration won for the simple, practical reason that nature, as it were, was calling.

So she caterpillared her way out of her downy sleeping bag, pulled her hiking shorts on over the black, fleecy leggings she'd slept in, zipped up her polar fleece jumper, crammed her grandmother's knitted beanie over her brown hair, and pushed her way outside.

The other tent was gone. For a moment, that made her pulse race—but then the reality of her surroundings overtook her senses. The air inside the tent had been warm, musty. The air outside yesterday had smelled of the sea, a salty tang with just a hint of rotting seaweed.

Today, the air smelled like sap, and living things, a green smell she associated with her grandmother's garden thanks to that summer she'd spent there when she was twelve, when they'd spent hours of days of weeks pruning and twining and tending, returning to the house only for meals and sleep, hands crusty with black dirt her grandmother called gold, under-nails caked with the stuff, elbows and knees stained black—and green.

This, Deena thought, was what every green scratch-and-sniff thing should smell like. Forget your apple, forget your lime; *this* was green. She inhaled deeply, and despite the oddity of the situation, felt her eyes light up as her body relaxed, melting into the space while at the same time inflated, buoyed, full. Something about this wondrous, spontaneous forest was familiar—and right.

She had no idea what the trees were, but they were tall, straight as ship masts or indigenous spears, thick and thin, rough-barked but paler than stringy barks, a brownish-grey, and the tiny, emerald, coin-sized leaves looked soft as butter, soft as petals.

Deena had tried keeping plants in their third-floor apartment back home, but somehow she could never remember to water them enough, or else she watered them too much and they died, thin and pustulant. She cried, every time, as her mother shook her head and made Deena walk them down to the communal skip bins in the alleyway behind the complex.

Her grandmother had consoled her on the phone each time, had promised that one day she'd have plants aplenty, more than she knew what to do with.

But one day wasn't soon enough for Deena—which was why she'd taken up hiking, of course. If she couldn't have plants at home, by golly was she going to surround herself with them in her spare time. So a forest? Amazing.

The other tent, her friends, vanishing? Less so.

Nature was still calling.

And the current cover situation was a little thin for her liking; yesterday, there'd been a handy thicket of salt bushes and something vaguely acacia-like between the grass and the sand dunes. Today, it was just open forest all the way down to the sand behind and to her right, and all the way up to the mountains ahead and to the left.

On the other hand, there didn't seem to be anyone else around.

Sighing, she attended to her body's needs, butt cheeks momentarily icing over as a wind whipped down from the mountain, setting the trees rushling and shushling—but it seemed like a freak gust and nothing more, and soon enough she was clothed and warm again—and hungry.

A brief forage in the tent revealed a couple of muesli bars tucked into the pocket of her raincoat, and of course, there were the packet soups in her hiking pack, and she still had a couple of litres of water.

Nothing to heat it with, though; Rachel had had the Trangia in her pack, and sometime in the night—as was pretty usual, these days—she'd snuck into the boys' tent, taking her pack with her for a pillow.

Which meant that all of the above—Rachel, boys, tent, packs, and cooking stove—were now gone.

Deena sat heavily on the stump by

the front of the tent and dropped her chin into her hands.

It wasn't that she'd never believed in magic before—she'd seen her grandmother's garden after all, and although she'd stopped protesting to the contrary so people would stop protesting her sanity, she knew full well she'd seen creatures in her grandmother's garden when she'd been little that had no right existing on this mortal plane.

But on the other hand, until now, magic had been content to merely linger in the background, a blurred, bokehed backdrop to real life, something vaguely sensed, but never fully realised.

What, Deena wondered, had made the difference today? Why now suddenly jump arrestingly into the foreground?

Or, she wondered, gazing around as the trees whispered secretively, why *here*?

Hmm.

That seemed like a crucial question.

The tent, she felt, was light enough. It would be a bit of a headache to get the whole thing into her pack with her camping mat—yesterday, Rachel had been carrying half the tent, but that clearly wasn't an option today, and neither was leaving the tent behind—but she should be able to manage.

Because as she saw it, she could either sit here all day, hoping and wondering whether the others would come back—or she could go explore this magical, magical forest that even now was layering calm over her like blankets, like she belonged here, and *find out* what had happened to the others.

It took about thirty minutes, moving purposefully, to down a couple of muesli bars, swirl a packet of soup into one of the water bottles and gag it down, and pack up all the gear. It did fit in her pack—only just, and she'd had to let all the straps out, but it wasn't too heavy, just bulky.

And so, with the legs zipped onto her hiking shorts, turning them into pants once more, with her heavy boots on and her beanie still crammed over her hair and her hands deep in the pockets of her emerald-green polar fleece jumper, and her dark blue pack sticking up over her head and weighing down her hips, Deena set off through the trees that had miraculously appeared, heading back approximately the way they'd come in the evening before.

The Australian bush was always fairly quiet, so it was some time before Deena realised quite how unnaturally quiet the scene actually was; she was, without exaggeration, the only thing making any sound, if you discounted the still-audible hush of the ocean and the sporadic rustling of the trees when the breeze picked up. No birdsong, no rustling of small animals that she could detect...

Nothing.

It didn't worry her as much as it might have, the bush being as afore-mentioned a relatively quiet place anyway, but it was certainly something to note.

Yesterday, they'd come in around the mountain from the south, joining a track at its feet that followed the coastline north to the little cleared area they'd used as a camp. The air had tasted of salt and smelled like teatree as they'd pushed their way onto the narrow dirt track amid the tussocky grass.

Today, there were no teatree thickets, and although Deena had her map and compass and was perfectly adept in using them both, she still felt uneasy striking off the path into the midst of the unknown, with nary a familiar landmark in sight.

That was, of course, except for the mountain. She glanced up at it, with her back to the ocean as she stood somewhere around the point where they'd joined the track yesterday—she knew that because there was the rocky promontory behind her, a tiny stub sticking out into the water no more than ten or twenty metres, but clearly once a lot more impressive because of the small chain of rocky little islands that led out from it.

It was a beast of a mountain, steep and covered in boulders and drop-offs—a fact now largely obscured by the monotonous, tall, straight trees of the spontaneous forest, but a fact nonetheless.

Still. Deena couldn't help but think that if she could somehow get to the top of the mountain, she might be able to get a better handle on whatever was going on.

Certainly, it was a surer route than

striking off the path at random. And at least if she was going *up,* she couldn't get lost, spontaneous forest aside.

The fact that something in the forest seemed to be directing her that way, that the chill wind earlier had seemed to come from up there, that had nothing to do with it, of course. All she was after was the view, so she could determine how far this new, strange forest stretched, and see what she could do about getting out of it to find her friends.

And so, up the mountain she went.

Keep reading! Head to
**www.inkprintpress.com/
amylaurens/forests/**
to buy your copy now!

INKLETS

Collect them all! Released on the 1st and 15th of each month.

INKLET #055
Allure
AMY LAURENS

INKLET #056
The LIES We KNOW
LIANA BROOKS

DOUBLE ISSUE
INKLET #057
AFTERMATH & Fool Me Once
AMY LAURENS

INKLET #058
Purity
An Age Of Unicorns Story
AMY LAURENS

INKLET #059
Saved
AMY LAURENS

INKLET #060
A Kiss is the Secret
AMY LAURENS

INKLET #061
A Cleansing Tides Story
Fire Bright
AMY LAURENS

INKLET #062
Hades AND Persephone
LIANA BROOKS

INKLET #063
Just So Long As You're Happy
AMY LAURENS

INKLET #064
Theft Of A Lifetime
LIANA BROOKS

INKLET #065
Shoe
AMY LAURENS

INKLET #066
Published AUTHOR
LIANA BROOKS

DOUBLE ISSUE
INKLET #067
THE REMARKABLE INSIGHT OF JELLYBEANS & Understanding
AMY LAURENS

INKLET #068
Desperate Measures
AMY LAURENS

INKLET #069
Rock-a-bye
LIANA BROOKS

INKLET #070
the Other Carly
AMY LAURENS

INKLET #071
By By Bioluminescent Light
AMY LAURENS

INKLET #072
Even Villains Grant Wishes
A Heroes & Villains Story
LIANA BROOKS

www.ingramcontent.com/pod-product-compliance
Lightning Source LLC
Chambersburg PA
CBHW032052180726
48284CB00004B/1297